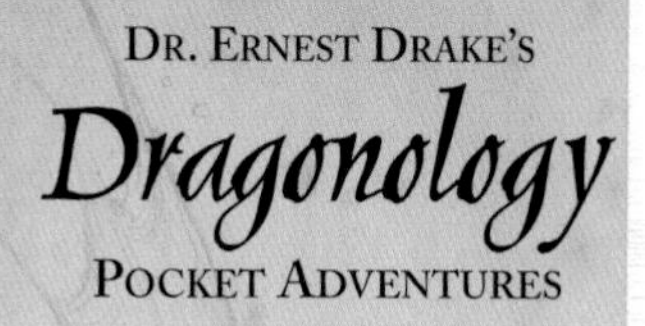

THE DRAGON ST

EDITED BY
DUGALD A. STEER, B.A. (BRIST), S.A.S.D.

Ernest Drake

THE TEMPLAR COMPANY:
PUBLISHERS OF RARE & UNUSUAL BOOKS.

Kingdom of Norway
Kingdom of Sweden
United Kingdom
Kingdom of Denmark
Empire of Russia
London
German Realm
Belgium
Prague
Empire of Austria
Kingdom of Hungary
French Republic
Switzerland
Reutte
Klagenfurt
Kingdom of Italy
Portugal
Kingdom of Spain
EUROPE
1877
SPECIAL EQUIPMENT LIST
Flame-proof cloak and hat; English guineas; Austrian schillings; Clothes and make-up to disguise yourself; A letter with the seal of the S.A.S.D. and Dr. Drake's signature; German phrase book; Czech phrase book

Welcome to Dr. Drake's

DRAGON STAR ADVENTURE!

You are a keen member of the *Secret and Ancient Society of Dragonologists*. Learning about dragons is your passion, and you particularly enjoy field work. So you are very pleased to receive another special dragonological mission from Dr. Ernest Drake.

The Secret and Ancient Society of Dragonologists

DRAGONOLOGICAL MISSION

Date: 1st June 1880 Location: England/Austrian Empire

Mission: Dark Dragonologists are searching for the Dragon Star - a powerful gem said to have been taken to Prague by the Elizabethan dragonologist Dr. Dee. You must locate the gem before they do!

DR. DEE used to live in Mortlake, a village near London. You decide to start looking for clues there, but when you arrive you find that Dee's house was knocked down years ago. It is now a building site. The foreman tells you that his men have unearthed some unusual things from a strange underground room, which they sold to a local antique dealer. The dealer shows you the items. He will take 10 guineas each for them. One is a very old book marked *Pryvate*. The other is a sealed casket with three pictures engraved on it: there's a cat pawing at a very similar-looking casket, a mechanical lizard-thing coming out, and a cat running for its life. You only have 12 guineas.

You must make a decision. Do you:

A. Buy the book marked *Pryvate.* [go to **13**]

B. Buy the sealed iron casket. Perhaps the Dragon Star is inside? [go to **14**]

2 You wonder if the Dragon Star is protected by a dragon. You visit the town museum where there is supposed to be a dragon skull. It turns out to be the skull of an extinct rhino, but the curator tells you that there was a real dragon and that it moved to a town called Reutte years before. [go to **18**].

3 In the tower room it does not take very long to find a fireplace with alphabetical letters on it. Quickly you search it until you find a brick that has a tiny "D" in one corner. But just as you are about to press the brick you hear voices coming from the other side of the wall. Do you:

A. Press the brick anyway. [go to **11**]

B. Decide to look round some more. [go to **27**]

4

The angry dragon does not seem happy at all. In fact she lets out a roar of rage. Then she rears up and draws back her huge tail, using it to give you a tremendous blow that sends you flying. She lashes you again and again with her tail until you earnestly wish you had never ever heard of dragons and...

YOUR TALE ENDS AT A TAIL'S END!

5 The night starts to get colder and colder. As you have not brought any blankets you start to shiver. No one seems to have arrived, and the barrels are stacked on the opposite wall of the keep, so you now have a choice to make. Do you:

A. Decide that you will just have to put up with the cold. [go to **10**]

B. Light a nice, warming fire. [go to **21**]

6 The narrow path twists and turns until it comes out on a narrow ledge under the keep. It leads to a tunnel that goes under the castle. As you start to go up the tunnel, you set off a tripwire that causes a huge boulder to roll down the tunnel towards you. You cannot escape, and so...

YOU ARE COMPLETELY SQUISHED!

7 The mob do not see you, and after a while they move on. To warm up you decide to explore the ruins by moonlight. In one chamber you find a pit, with a loose wooden cover. Do you:

A. Go and ask the villagers if the pit is dangerous to climb into. [go to **20**]

B. Immediately climb into the pit. [go to **35**]

8 The wicked dragonologists smile. One pulls a lever and a trapdoor opens up below your feet. You fall into a lost dungeon beneath the laboratory where you find the ghost of Dr. Faustus, who is still haunting the house. "I did it for science," says the ghost again and again until, although you are trapped without food or water...

YOU ARE BORED TO DEATH!

9 You arrive at the Faust House, but it seems to be locked up. There's a sign on the door which says, "Open 10 until 4". Your watch says a quarter to four. Luckily you look like a pretty ordinary tourist, and so the guard reluctantly allows you in. "There have been some very strange noises coming from the tower room," he explains. You look quite interested, as he points the way to the room. [go to **3**]

10 Soon you forget about the cold because you hear a mob of angry villagers from Reutte, bringing torches. One of them shouts, "Look! I can see the barrels!" Do you:

A. Try to hide from them. [go to **7**]

B. Decide to talk to them. [go to **20**]

11 The fireplace swings open to reveal an ancient laboratory. Two people are pondering over some runes. They are dark dragonologists! Do you:

A. Cry, "Leave at once, or else show me your dragonological licenses!" [go to **8**]

B. Pretend to be a tourist who pressed the brick by accident, and go back out. [go to **25**]

12 As soon as you answer, the dragon flies away, so you cannot ask any more about the Dragon Star. You carry on up through the trees until you come to a fork in the road. There are two possible ways towards the castle. Do you:

A. Go left, along a thorny, narrow path. [go to **6**]

B. Go right, along the broad, easy way. [go to **29**]

13 As soon as you open the book you see there is a whole chapter on the Dragon Star. But the vital clue is in code! Luckily you know the code: it is the same one used by Mary, Queen of Scots, during the "Babington Plot".

a b c d e f g h i j k l m

n o p q r s t u v w x y z

the in by

It is time for a trip across Europe! Do you:

A. Decide to visit Prague first. [go to **15**]

B. Go to Klagenfurt immediately. [go to **31**]

14 You lose no time in opening the casket, but realise your mistake, when TEN mechanical lizards crawl out, snapping their metal jaws and running up your trouser leg. There's no escape! And just as the mechanical lizard guardians start to nibble in earnest, you realise the picture on the casket was actually a horrible warning, because...

CURIOSITY KILLED THE CAT!

15 In Prague, you take a room in the Wenceslas Hotel. You know that Dr. Dee once lived for a short time in Prague, in a place now known as the "Faust House", but you don't know where that is. Do you:

A. Order a cab and say, "Faust House!" [go to **9**]

B. Take the advice of the hotel porter, and ask the way at a local inn. [go to **34**]

16 Entering the lair, you see the dragon curled around the Dragon Star, her chicks nearby. You show her a letter from Dr. Drake. Do you:

A. Cry, "You were protector of the Star, but I must look after it now. Give it to me!" [go to **30**]

B. Cry, "Beware! I think someone is planning to blow up the castle and steal the star!" [go to **33**]

17 Hiding in the woods, you hear angry voices, shouting, "Someone has disturbed the dragon!" Next, you see a large group of people who are all carrying torches and pitchforks. They are townspeople from Reutte, and they seem very angry indeed about something. Do you:

A. Stay absolutely still and quiet. [go to **7**]

B. Decide to talk to them. [go to **20**]

18 You go to Reutte, and decide to look for dragons up by the old Ehrenburg castle ruins. Suddenly, a huge red dragon appears. "Tell me the secret word and you may pass," she cries. "But you must leave before nightfall!" Do you:

A. Cry, "Rapunzel is the word!" [go to **4**]

B. Cry, "Rumpelstiltskin is the word!" [go to **12**]

19 The dragon smiles, and stares right into your eyes. You are surprised just how very charming and wonderful the dragon seems. "Come with me," she says, which feels like a good idea. You go with the dragon to her lair, where its chicks are waiting. You feel like stroking them. But you have been hypnotised, and...

YOU ARE CHOMPED BY THE CHICKS!

20 The torch-bearing mob do not give you a chance to speak. "Get him!" they cry. "He has made our dragon very angry!" You must run as fast as you can. Do you:

A. Head to the cliff, and climb down. [go to **26**]
B. Run to the castle, where you find a room with a sort of pit in it that you can hide in. [go to **35**]

21 The fire crackles and blazes, and as you start to warm up, you begin to feel a lot more cheerful. You realise the wicked dragonologists must have left the barrels, planning to blow their way into the dragon's lair beneath. But at that moment a gust of wind carries a spark over towards the barrels, and...

YOU ARE BLOWN TO SMITHEREENS!

22 The tunnel comes out by the castle wall. The voices you heard were coming from the two dark dragonologists, who are fiddling with a long fuse near the barrels of gunpowder. "We'll blow a way into the dragon's lair!" laughs one. Do you:

A. Turn around and head for the lair. [go to **16**]

B. Wait and see what happens. [go to **37**]

23 The angry mob are hot on your heels as you run towards the river. There is no escape. Soon you find yourself hoisted up and thrown headlong into the Danube. You pull yourself out on the other bank. Do you:

A. Return to London to fetch a dragon-whistle, then head straight to Klagenfurt. [go to **31**]

B. Go to your hotel to dry off. [go to **36**]

24 The dragon returns. "The evil dragonologists will not bother us again," she says. "I thank you for keeping my chicks safe." The dragon explains that one of her ancestors, the Klagenfurt Lindworm, was given the Dragon Star gem by Dr. Dee, but moved to Ehrenburg when too many tourists began investigating dragon tales after a fossilised rhinoceros skull was found. [go to **38**]

25 As soon as you are outside the room again, you write down the runes, which you managed to commit to memory. It is surprising that the dark dragonologists didn't seem to understand them, but as a *bona fide* member of the Dr. Ernest Drake's S.A.S.D. you shouldn't have any trouble at all.

ᚦᛖ ᛞᚱᚪᚷᚩᚾ ᚹᚩᚱᛞ
ᚩᚻ ᛚᛁᛏᛏᛚᛖ ᛣᚾᚩᚹ ᛏᚻᛖ ᚳᚩᛗᛗᚩᚾ ᚻᛖᚱᛞ
ᛏᚻᚪᛏ ᚱᚢᛗᛈᛖᛚᛋᛏᛁᛚᛏᛋᛣᛁᚾ ᛁᛋ ᛏᚻᛖ ᚹᚩᚱᛞ

Dragon Script:

ᚠ	F	ᚷ	G	ᛇ	Ï	ᛖ	E	ᚪ	A
ᚢ	U/V	ᚹ	W	ᛈ	P	ᛗ	M	ᚫ	Æ
ᚦ	Th	ᚻ	H	ᛉ	X/Z	ᛚ	L	ᚣ	Y
ᚩ	O	ᚾ	N	ᛋ	S	ᛝ	Ng	ᛠ	EA
ᚱ	R	ᛁ	I	ᛏ	T	ᛟ	Œ	ᚸ	Gh
ᚳ	C	ᛄ	J	ᛒ	B	ᛞ	D	ᛣ	K

Now you know the secret word, it is time to go to Klagenfurt and find the Dragon Star! [go to **2**]

26 Halfway down the cliff you see the dragon, waiting for you at the bottom. The dragon shouts, "I told you to be gone by nightfall!" Do you:

A. Cry, "I apologise, but I was sent here to protect the Dragon Star." [go to **19**]

B. Cry, "Those people on the cliff are trying to steal the Dragon Star!" [go to **32**]

27 The Faust House is very interesting, but apart from the odd pestle and mortar and two framed pictures, there are very few antiquities left from 1584 when Dr. Dee and his assistant Kelly stayed in it, doing experiments to try and discover the lost Philosopher's Stone. Do you:

A. Go back and press the brick. [go to **11**]

B. Look round some more. [go to **27**]

28 As you escape with the Dragon Star, it begins to glow brighter and brighter, and makes a high-pitched whining noise, which soon brings the dragon. "I was a fool to trust a young human such as you!" it roars. Without your flame-proof cloak you don't stand a chance, and you soon... **SIZZLE TO A BLACKENED CINDER!**

29 The broad road leads into the main gate of the castle keep. You see a stack of barrels that are filled with gunpowder. Could the dark dragonologists have got here first? Do you:

A. Hide by the barrels, to see if anyone comes near them. [go to **5**]

B. Hide in the woods nearby. [go to **17**]

30 "No human shall touch the Dragon Star!" cries the dragon. Despite a sudden gigantic explosion, which rocks the lair to its foundations, and causes what is left of the castle walls far above you to collapse, the dragon leaps at you, attacking you with her claws, wrenching and tearing and clawing and gnawing until...

YOU ARE TOTALLY SHREDDED!

31 First, you borrow a dragon-whistle from the S.A.S.D and, after a long journey, finally arrive near the town of Klagenfurt. You blow the whistle. After an hour or two a dragon arrives, looking very angry. Do you:

A. Cry, "I seek the Dragon Star!" [go to **4**]

B. Decide you'd had really better unearth any clues in Prague first. [go to **15**]

32 You are trapped. If you try to climb down, the dragon will blast a jet of fire in your direction, but if you climb back up again, then the angry mob are sure to spear you on the ends of their pitchforks. There is no way out at all. Your only choice now is to decide which grizzly, unpleasant and nasty end you would prefer to meet...

FIRE OR PITCHFORKS? IT'S UP TO YOU!

33 The dragon nods and says, "I will trust you because you are a friend of Dr. Drake." She flies off, leaving you with her chicks. You are very worried in case there is an explosion. Do you:

A. Use your flame-proof cloak to protect the dragon chicks. [go to **24**]

B. Take the Dragon Star for safekeeping, leaving the flame-proof cloak in exchange. [go to **28**]

34 As soon as you arrive at the Inn, you ask for directions to the Faust House, and explain about your interest in Dr. Dee. But the very minute that you do this, you find yourself in the middle of a mob of angry locals, who start to chase you through the streets. "We don't want any more dragons or occult nonsense round here!"

they cry. "We have had enough of that sort of thing!" Do you:

A. Run down a street towards the river. [go to **23**]

B. Try and run back to your hotel. [go to **36**]

35 The pit must at one time have been the old dungeon of the castle, and even now it is filled with skulls, bones and bits of torn cloth. However, two tunnels have been dug into it. Hot air from the one on the right suggests that it is going to be the way to the dragon's lair, while you can hear loud voices coming from the tunnel on the left. Do you:

A. Take the tunnel that seems to be heading towards the dragon's lair. [go to **16**]

B. Take the left-hand tunnel. [go to **22**]

36 Back at the hotel, the concierge explains that strange noises have been heard coming from behind a fireplace in the tower of the Faust House. Even though the building has been rebuilt since Dee's time, it still makes some locals jumpy, especially since two "dragon experts" started to take a very keen interest in it. [go to **9**]

37 What happens is that the two evil dragonologists retreat to a safe distance, and light the fuse. The spark races up the fuse, and ignites the barrels, which all blow up. The explosion is so vast that it knocks down a huge part of the castle wall. This just happens to be the part you are underneath. So you...

GET IN A SPOT OF RUBBLE TROUBLE!

38 The dragon then takes the Dragon Star in one of her claws and shows it to you. It has a dull light inside. "It glows brightly whenever people with evil intent are near!" she says. "Now you have found the Star, you may tell Dr. Drake that I will guard it and that it is safe. If he would like to come and see it here he is welcome. I would very much like to meet him one day."

Congratulations!

This is to certify that

----

has survived the difficulties of the
Dragon Star Adventure.
You have succeeded admirably!
Dr. Drake
is proud of your
Dragonological Achievement!!

Ernest Drake